My Birthday

By Heather Hammonds

My Birthday

I had a party for my birthday.

My friends
came to my party.
We had fun!

Party Games

We played party games
in the yard.
We sat in a circle.

At the Table

Mom and Dad made the party food.

We sat at the big table to eat our food.

We all got a party hat!

The Party Food

We had lots of party food.

We had:

- party bread
- chips
- cheese and crackers
- fruit
- cupcakes
- green gelatin

Cupcakes

I had a yellow cupcake.

Emily had a pink cupcake.

Thomas had a blue cupcake.

Lots of Fruit

We had lots of fruit to eat.

We liked the fruit!

My Birthday Cake

I had a big birthday cake.

My birthday cake looked very good.

I had six candles on my cake.

Good-bye

After my party,

I said good-bye to my friends.

I liked my birthday party.

I had fun!